Count Lev Nikolayevich Tolstoy (9 September [O.S. 28 August] 1828 – 20 November [O.S. 7 November] 1910), usually referred to in English as Leo Tolstoy, was a Russian writer who is regarded as one of the greatest authors of all time. He received multiple nominations for Nobel Prize in Literature every year from 1902 to 1906, and nominations for Nobel Peace Prize in 1901, 1902 and 1910, and his miss of the prize is a major Nobel prize controversy. Born to an aristocratic Russian family in 1828, he is best known for the novels War and Peace (1869) and Anna Karenina (1877), often cited as pinnacles of realist fiction. He first achieved literary acclaim in his twenties with his semi-autobiographical trilogy, Childhood, Boyhood, and Youth (1852–1856), and Sevastopol Sketches (1855), based upon his experiences in the Crimean War. Tolstoy's fiction includes dozens of short stories and several novellas such as The Death of Ivan Ilyich (1886), Family Happiness (1859), and Hadji Murad (1912). He also wrote plays and numerous philosophical essays. (Source: Wikipedia)

Literary works:

The Autobiographical Trilogy

Childhood (1852)

Boyhood (1854)

Youth (1856)

War and Peace (1869)

Anna Karenina (1877)

Resurrection (1899)

Family Happiness (1859)

The Cossacks (1863)

The Death of Ivan Ilyich (1886)

The Kreutzer Sonata (1889)

The Devil (1911)

The Forged Coupon (1911)

Hadji Murat (1917)

THRONE CLASSICS

WHERE LOVE IS THERE GOD IS ALSO

LEO TOLSTOY

THRONE CLASSICS

This is a work of fiction. Names, characters, places, and incidents either are the product of the author's imagination or are used fictitiously. Any resemblance to actual persons, living or dead, events, or locales is entirely coincidental.

First Printing: 2019

ISBN 978-93-5383-007-6 (paperback)

ISBN 978-93-5383-008-3 (Hardcover)

ISBN 978-93-5383-009-0 (eBook)

Published by Throne Classics

www.throneclassics.com

Contents

WHERE LOVE IS THERE GOD IS ALSO

WHERE LOVE IS THERE GOD IS ALSO

IN the city lived the shoemaker, Martuin Avdyeitch. He lived in a basement, in a little room with one window. The window looked out on the street. Through the window he used to watch the people passing by; although only their feet could be seen, yet by the boots, Martuin Avdyeitch recognized the people. Martuin Avdyeitch had lived long in one place, and had many acquaintances. Few pairs of boots in his district had not been in his hands once and again. Some he would half-sole, some he would patch, some he would stitch around, and occasionally he would also put on new uppers. And through the window he often recognized his work.

Avdyeitch had plenty to do, because he was a faithful workman, used good material, did not make exorbitant charges, and kept his word. If it was possible for him to finish an order by a certain time, he would accept it; otherwise, he would not deceive you,—he would tell you so beforehand. And all knew Avdyeitch, and he was never out of work.

Avdyeitch had always been a good man; but as he grew old, he began to think more about his soul, and get nearer to God. Martuin's wife had died when he was still living with his master. His wife left him a boy three years old. None of their other children had lived. All the eldest had died in childhood. Martuin at first intended to send his little son to his sister in the village, but afterward he felt sorry for him; he thought to himself:—

"It will be hard for my Kapitoshka to live in a strange family. I shall keep him with me."

And Avdyeitch left his master, and went into lodgings with his little son. But God gave Avdyeitch no luck with his children. As Kapitoshka grew older, he began to help his father, and would have been a delight to him, but a sickness fell on him, he went to bed, suffered a week, and died. Martuin buried his son, and fell into despair. So deep was this despair that he began to complain of God. Martuin fell into such a melancholy state, that more than once he prayed to God for death, and reproached God because He had not taken him who was an old man, instead of his beloved only son. Avdyeitch also ceased to go to church.

And once a little old man from the same district came from Troïtsa(1) to see Avdyeitch; for seven years he had been wandering about. Avdyeitch talked with him, and began to complain about his sorrows.

"I have no desire to live any longer," he said, "I only wish I was dead. That is all I pray God for. I am a man without anything to hope for now."

And the little old man said to him:—

"You don't talk right, Martuin, we must not judge God's doings. The world moves, not by our skill, but by God's will. God decreed for your son to die,—for you—to live. So it is for the best. And you are in despair, because you wish to live for your own happiness."

"But what shall one live for?" asked Martuin.

And the little old man said:—

"We must live for God, Martuin. He gives you life, and for His sake you must live. When you begin to live for Him, you will not grieve over anything, and all will seem easy to you."

Martuin kept silent for a moment, and then said, "But how can one live for God?"

And the little old man said:—

"Christ has taught us how to live for God. You know how to read? Buy a Testament, and read it; there you will learn how to live for God. Everything is explained there."

And these words kindled a fire in Avdyeitch's heart. And he went that very same day, bought a New Testament in large print, and began to read.

At first Avdyeitch intended to read only on holidays; but as he began to read, it so cheered his soul that he used to read every day. At times he would become so absorbed in reading, that all the kerosene in the lamp would burn out, and still he could not tear himself away. And so Avdyeitch used to read every evening.

And the more he read, the clearer he understood what God wanted of him, and how one should live for God; and his heart kept growing easier and easier. Formerly, when he lay down to sleep, he used to sigh and groan, and always thought of his Kapitoshka; and now his only exclamation was:—

"Glory to Thee! glory to Thee, Lord! Thy will be done."

And from that time Avdyeitch's whole life was changed. In other days he, too, used to drop into a public-house(2) as a holiday amusement, to drink a cup of tea; and he was not averse to a little brandy, either. He would take a drink with some acquaintance, and leave the saloon, not intoxicated, exactly, yet in a happy frame of mind, and inclined to talk nonsense, and shout, and use abusive language at a person. Now he left off that sort of thing. His life became quiet and joyful. In the morning he would sit down to work, finish his allotted task, then take the little lamp from the hook, put it on the table, get his book from the shelf, open it, and sit down to read. And the more he read, the more he understood, and the brighter and happier it grew in his heart.

Once it happened that Martuin read till late into the night. He was reading the Gospel of Luke. He was reading over the sixth chapter; and he was reading the verses:—

"And unto him that smiteth thee on the one cheek offer also the other; and him that taketh away thy cloak forbid not to take thy coat also. Give to every man that asketh of thee; and of him that taketh away thy goods ask them not again. And as ye would that men should do to you, do ye also to them likewise."

He read farther also those verses, where God speaks:

"And why call ye me, Lord, Lord, and do not the things which I say? Whosoever cometh to me, and heareth my sayings, and doeth them, I will shew you to whom he is like: he is like a man which built an house, and digged deep, and laid the foundation on a rock: and when the flood arose, the stream beat

vehemently upon that house, and could not shake it; for it was founded upon a rock. But he that heareth, and doeth not, is like a man that without a foundation built an house upon the earth; against which the stream did beat vehemently, and immediately it fell; and the ruin of that house was great."

Avdyeitch read these words, and joy filled his soul. He took off his spectacles, put them down on the book, leaned his elbows on the table, and became lost in thought. And he began to measure his life by these words. And he thought to himself:—

"Is my house built on the rock, or on the sand? 'Tis well if on the rock. It is so easy when you are alone by yourself; it seems as if you had done everything as God commands; but when you forget yourself, you sin again. Yet I shall still struggle on. It is very good. Help me, Lord!"

Thus ran his thoughts; he wanted to go to bed, but he felt loath to tear himself away from the book. And he began to read farther in the seventh chapter. He read about the centurion, he read about the widow's son, he read about the answer given to John's disciples, and finally he came to that place where the rich Pharisee desired the Lord to sit at meat with him; and he read how the woman that was a sinner anointed His feet, and washed them with her tears, and how He forgave her. He reached the forty-fourth verse, and began to read:—

"And he turned to the woman, and said unto Simon, Seest thou this woman? I entered into thine house, thou gavest me no water for my feet: but she hath washed my feet with tears, and wiped them with the hairs of her head. Thou gavest me no kiss: but this woman since the time I came in hath not ceased to kiss my feet. My head with oil thou didst not anoint: but this woman hath anointed my feet with ointment."

He finished reading these verses, and thought to himself:—

"Thou gavest me no water for my feet, thou gavest me no kiss. My head with oil thou didst not anoint."

And again Avdyeitch took off his spectacles, put them down on the book, and again he became lost in thought.

"It seems that Pharisee must have been such a man as I am. I, too, apparently have thought only of myself,—how I might have my tea, be warm and comfortable, but never to think about my guest. He thought about himself, but there was not the least care taken of the guest. And who was his guest? The Lord Himself. If He had come to me, should I have done the same way?"

Avdyeitch rested his head upon both his arms, and did not notice that he fell asleep.

"Martuin!" suddenly seemed to sound in his ears.

Martuin started from his sleep:—

"Who is here?"

He turned around, glanced toward the door—no one.

Again he fell into a doze. Suddenly, he plainly heard:—

"Martuin! Ah, Martuin! look to-morrow on the street. I am coming."

Martuin awoke, rose from the chair, began to rub his eyes. He himself could not tell whether he heard those words in his dream, or in reality. He turned down his lamp, and went to bed.

At daybreak next morning, Avdyeitch rose, made his prayer to God, lighted the stove, put on the shchi(3) and the kasha,(4) put the water in the samovar, put on his apron, and sat down by the window to work.

And while he was working, he kept thinking about all that had happened the day before. It seemed to him at one moment that it was a dream, and now he had really heard a voice.

"Well," he said to himself, "such things have been."

Martuin was sitting by the window, and looking out more than he was working. When anyone passed by in boots which he did not know, he would bend down, look out of the window, in order to see, not only the feet, but also the face.

The dvornik(5) passed by in new felt boots,(6) the water-carrier passed by; then there came up to the window an old soldier of Nicholas's time, in an old pair of laced felt boots, with a shovel in his hands. Avdyeitch recognized him by his felt boots. The old man's name was Stepanuitch; and a neighboring merchant, out of charity, gave him a home with him. He was required to assist the dvornik. Stepanuitch began to shovel away the snow from in front of Avdyeitch's window. Avdyeitch glanced at him, and took up his work again.

"Pshaw! I must be getting crazy in my old age," said Avdyeitch, and laughed at himself. "Stepanuitch is clearing away the snow, and I imagine that Christ is coming to see me. I was entirely out of my mind, old dotard that I am!"

Avdyeitch sewed about a dozen stitches, and then felt impelled to look through the window again. He looked out again through the window, and saw that Stepanuitch had leaned his shovel against the wall, and was warming himself, and resting. He was an old, broken-down man; evidently he had not strength enough even to shovel the snow. Avdyeitch said to himself:—

"I will give him some tea; by the way, the samovar has only just gone out." Avdyeitch laid down his awl, rose from his seat, put the samovar on the table, poured out the tea, and tapped with his finger at the glass. Stepanuitch turned around, and came to the window. Avdyeitch beckoned to him, and went to open the door.

"Come in, warm yourself a little," he said. "You must be cold."

"May Christ reward you for this! my bones ache," said Stepanuitch.

Stepanuitch came in, and shook off the snow, tried to wipe his feet, so as not to soil the floor, but staggered.

"Don't trouble to wipe your feet. I will clean it up myself; we are used to such things. Come in and sit down," said Avdyeitch. "Here, drink a cup of tea."

And Avdyeitch lifted two glasses, and handed one to his guest; while he himself poured his tea into a saucer, and began to blow it.

Stepanuitch finished drinking his glass of tea, turned the glass upside down,(7) put the half-eaten lump of sugar on it, and began to express his thanks. But it was evident he wanted some more.

"Have some more," said Avdyeitch, filling both his own glass and his guest's. Avdyeitch drank his tea, but from time to time glanced out into the street.

"Are you expecting anyone?" asked his guest.

"Am I expecting anyone? I am ashamed even to tell whom I expect. I am, and I am not, expecting someone; but one word has kindled a fire in my heart. Whether it is a dream, or something else, I do not know. Don't you see, brother, I was reading yesterday the Gospel about Christ the Batyushka; how He suffered, how He walked on the earth. I suppose you have heard about it?"

"Indeed I have," replied Stepanuitch; "but we are people in darkness, we can't read."

"Well, now, I was reading about that very thing,—how He walked on the earth; I read, you know, how He came to the Pharisee, and the Pharisee did not treat Him hospitably. Well, and so, my brother, I was reading yesterday, about this very thing, and was thinking to myself how he did not receive Christ, the Batyushka, with honor. Suppose, for example, He should come to me, or anyone else, I said to myself, I should not even know how to receive Him. And he gave Him no reception at all. Well! while I was thus thinking, I fell asleep, brother, and I heard someone call me by name. I got up; the voice, just as if someone whispered, said, 'Be on the watch; I shall come to-morrow.' And this happened twice. Well! would you believe it, it got into my head? I scolded myself—and yet I am expecting Him, the Batyushka."

Stepanuitch shook his head, and said nothing; he finished drinking his glass of tea, and put it on the side; but Avdyeitch picked up the glass again, and filled it once more.

"Drink some more for your good health. You see, I have an idea that, when the Batyushka went about on this earth, He disdained no one, and had more to do with the simple people. He always went to see the simple people.

He picked out His disciples more from among folk like such sinners as we are, from the working class. Said He, whoever exalts himself, shall be humbled, and he who is humbled shall become exalted. Said He, you call me Lord, and, said He, I wash your feet. Whoever wishes, said He, to be the first, the same shall be a servant to all. Because, said He, blessed are the poor, the humble, the kind, the generous."

And Stepanuitch forgot about his tea; he was an old man, and easily moved to tears. He was listening, and the tears rolled down his face.

"Come, now, have some more tea," said Avdyeitch; but Stepanuitch made the sign of the cross, thanked him, turned down his glass, and arose.

"Thanks to you," he says, "Martuin Avdyeitch, for treating me kindly, and satisfying me, soul and body."

"You are welcome; come in again; always glad to see a friend," said Avdyeitch.

Stepanuitch departed; and Martuin poured out the rest of the tea, drank it up, put away the dishes, and sat down again by the window to work, to stitch on a patch. He kept stitching away, and at the same time looking through the window. He was expecting Christ, and was all the while thinking of Him and His deeds, and his head was filled with the different speeches of Christ.

Two soldiers passed by: one wore boots furnished by the crown, and the other one, boots that he had made; then the master(8) of the next house passed by in shining galoshes; then a baker with a basket passed by. All passed by; and now there came also by the window a woman in woolen stockings and rustic bashmaks on her feet. She passed by the window, and stood still near the window-case.

Avdyeitch looked up at her from the window, and saw it was a stranger, a woman poorly clad, and with a child; she was standing by the wall with her back to the wind, trying to wrap up the child, and she had nothing to wrap it up in. The woman was dressed in shabby summer clothes; and from behind the frame, Avdyeitch could hear the child crying, and the woman trying to pacify it; but she was not able to pacify it.

Avdyeitch got up, went to the door, ascended the steps, and cried:—

"My good woman. Hey! my good woman!"(9)

The woman heard him and turned around.

"Why are you standing in the cold with the child? Come into my room, where it is warm; you can manage it better. Here, this way!"

The woman was astonished. She saw an old, old man in an apron, with spectacles on his nose, calling her to him. She followed him. They descended the steps and entered the room; the old man led the woman to his bed.

"There," says he, "sit down, my good woman, nearer to the stove; you can get warm, and nurse the little one."

"I have no milk for him. I myself have not eaten anything since morning," said the woman; but, nevertheless, she took the baby to her breast.

Avdyeitch shook his head, went to the table, brought out the bread and a dish, opened the oven door, poured into the dish some cabbage soup, took out the pot with the gruel, but it was not cooked as yet; so he filled the dish with shchi only, and put it on the table. He got the bread, took the towel down from the hook, and spread it upon the table.

"Sit down," he says, "and eat, my good woman; and I will mind the little one. You see, I once had children of my own; I know how to handle them."

The woman crossed herself, sat down at the table, and began to eat; while Avdyeitch took a seat on the bed near the infant. Avdyeitch kept smacking and smacking to it with his lips; but it was a poor kind of smacking, for he had no teeth. The little one kept on crying. And it occured to Avdyeitch to threaten the little one with his finger; he waved, waved his finger right before the child's mouth, and hastily withdrew it. He did not put it to its mouth, because his finger was black, and soiled with wax. And the little one looked at his finger, and became quiet; then it began to smile, and Avdyeitch also was glad. While the woman was eating, she told who she was, and whither she was going.

Said she:—

"I am a soldier's wife. It is now seven months since they sent my husband away off, and no tidings. I lived out as cook; the baby was born; no one cared to keep me with a child. This is the third month that I have been struggling along without a place. I ate up all I had. I wanted to engage as a wet-nurse—no one would take me—I am too thin, they say. I have just been to the merchant's wife, where lives a young woman I know, and so they promised to take us in. I thought that was the end of it. But she told me to come next week. And she lives a long way off. I got tired out; and it tired him, too, my heart's darling. Fortunately, our landlady takes pity on us for the sake of Christ, and gives us a room, else I don't know how I should manage to get along."

Avdyeitch sighed, and said:

"Haven't you any warm clothes?"

"Now is the time, friend, to wear warm clothes; but yesterday I pawned my last shawl for a twenty-kopek piece."(10)

The woman came to the bed, and took the child; and Avdyeitch rose, went to the partition, rummaged round, and succeeded in finding an old coat.

"Na!" says he; "It is a poor thing, yet you may turn it to some use."

The woman looked at the coat and looked at the old man; she took the coat, and burst into tears; and Avdyeitch turned away his head; crawling under the bed, he pushed out a little trunk, rummaged in it, and sat down again opposite the woman.

And the woman said:—

"May Christ bless you, little grandfather!(11) He must have sent me to your window. My little baby would have frozen to death. When I started out it was warm, but now it has grown cold. And He, the Batyushka, led you to look through the window and take pity on me, an unfortunate."

Avdyeitch smiled, and said:—

"Indeed, He did that! I have been looking through the window, my good woman, for some wise reason."

And Martuin told the soldier's wife his dream, and how he heard the voice,—how the Lord promised to come and see him that day.

"All things are possible," said the woman. She rose, put on the coat, wrapped up her little child in it; and, as she started to take leave, she thanked Avdyeitch again.

"Take this, for Christ's sake," said Avdyeitch, giving her a twenty-kopek piece; "redeem your shawl."

She made the sign of the cross, and Avdyeitch made the sign of the cross and went with her to the door.

The woman went away. Avdyeitch ate some shchi, washed the dishes, and sat down again to work. While he was working he still remembered the window; when the window grew darker he immediately looked out to see who was passing by. Acquaintances passed by and strangers passed by, and there was nothing out of the ordinary.

But here Avdyeitch saw that an old apple woman had stopped in front of his window. She carried a basket with apples. Only a few were left, as she had evidently sold them nearly all out; and over her shoulder she had a bag full of chips. She must have gathered them up in some new building, and was on her way home. One could see that the bag was heavy on her shoulder; she tried to shift it to the other shoulder. So she lowered the bag on the sidewalk, stood the basket with the apples on a little post, and began to shake down the splinters in the bag. And while she was shaking her bag, a little boy in a torn cap came along, picked up an apple from the basket, and was about to make his escape; but the old woman noticed it, turned around, and caught the youngster by his sleeve. The little boy began to struggle, tried to tear himself away; but the old woman grasped him with both hands, knocked off his cap, and caught him by the hair.

The little boy was screaming, the old woman was scolding. Avdyeitch lost no time in putting away his awl; he threw it upon the floor, sprang to the door,—he even stumbled on the stairs, and dropped his spectacles,—and rushed out into the street.

The old woman was pulling the youngster by his hair, and was scolding and threatening to take him to the policeman; the youngster was defending himself, and denying the charge.

"I did not take it," he said; "What are you licking me for? Let me go!"

Avdyeitch tried to separate them. He took the boy by his arm, and said:—

"Let him go, babushka; forgive him, for Christ's sake."

"I will forgive him so that he won't forget it till the new broom grows. I am going to take the little villain to the police."

Avdyeitch began to entreat the old woman:—

"Let him go, babushka," he said, "he will never do it again. Let him go, for Christ's sake."

The old woman let him loose; the boy started to run, but Avdyeitch kept him back.

"Ask the babushka's forgiveness," he said, "and don't you ever do it again; I saw you take the apple."

The boy burst into tears, and began to ask forgiveness.

"There now! that's right; and here's an apple for you."

And Avdyeitch took an apple from the basket, and gave it to the boy.

"I will pay you for it, babushka," he said to the old woman.

"You ruin them that way, the good-for-nothings," said the old woman. "He ought to be treated so that he would remember it for a whole week."

"Eh, babushka, babushka," said Avdyeitch, "that is right according to our judgment, but not according to God's. If he is to be whipped for an apple, then what ought to be done to us for our sins?"

The old woman was silent.

And Avdyeitch told her the parable of the master who forgave a debtor all that he owed him, and how the debtor went and began to choke one who owed him.

The old woman listened, and the boy stood listening.

"God has commanded us to forgive," said Avdyeitch, "else we, too, may not be forgiven. All should be forgiven, and the thoughtless especially."

The old woman shook her head, and sighed.

"That's so," said she; "but the trouble is that they are very much spoiled."

"Then we who are older must teach them," said Avdyeitch.

"That's just what I say," remarked the old woman. "I myself have had seven of them,—only one daughter is left."

And the old woman began to relate where and how she lived with her daughter, and how many grandchildren she had. "Here," she says, "my strength is only so-so, and yet I have to work. I pity the youngsters—my grandchildren—but what nice children they are! No one gives me such a welcome as they do. Aksintka won't go to anyone but me. 'Babushka, dear babushka, lovliest.'"

And the old woman grew quite sentimental.

"Of course, it is a childish trick. God be with him," said she, pointing to the boy.

The woman was just about to lift the bag up on her shoulder, when the boy ran up, and said:—

"Let me carry it, babushka; it is on my way."

The old woman nodded her head, and put the bag on the boy's back.

And side by side they passed along the street.

And the old woman even forgot to ask Avdyeitch to pay for the apple. Avdyeitch stood motionless, and kept gazing after them; and he heard them talking all the time as they walked away. After Avdyeitch saw them disappear, he returned to his room; he found his eye-glasses on the stairs,—they were not broken; he picked up his awl, and sat down to work again.

After working a little while, it grew darker, so that he could not see to sew; he saw the lamplighter passing by to light the street-lamps.

"It must be time to make a light," he said to himself; so he got his little lamp ready, hung it up, and he took himself again to his work. He had one boot already finished; he turned it around, looked at it: "Well done." He put away his tools, swept off the cuttings, cleared off the bristles and ends, took the lamp, set it on the table, and took down the Gospels from the shelf. He intended to open the book at the very place where he had yesterday put a piece of leather as a mark, but it happened to open at another place; and the moment Avdyeitch opened the Testament, he recollected his last night's dream. And as soon as he remembered it, it seemed as if he heard someone stepping about behind him. Avdyeitch looked around, and saw—there, in the dark corner, it seemed as if people were standing; he was at a loss to know who they were. And a voice whispered in his ear:—

"Martuin—ah, Martuin! did you not recognize me?"

"Who?" exclaimed Avdyeitch.

"Me," repeated the voice. "It was I;" and Stepanuitch stepped forth from the dark corner; he smiled, and like a little cloud faded away, and soon vanished.

"And it was I," said the voice.

From the dark corner stepped forth the woman with her child; the woman smiled, the child laughed, and they also vanished,

"And it was I," continued the voice; both the old woman and the boy with the apple stepped forward; both smiled and vanished.

Avdyeitch's soul rejoiced; he crossed himself, put on his spectacles, and began to read the Evangelists where it happened to open. On the upper part of the page he read:—

"For I was an hungered, and ye gave me meat; I was thirsty, and ye gave me drink; I was a stranger, and ye took me in."

And on the lower part of the page he read this:—

"Inasmuch as ye have done it unto one of the least of these my brethren, ye have done it unto me."—St. Matthew, Chap. xxv.

And Avdyeitch understood that his dream had not deceived him; that the Saviour really called on him that day, and that he really received Him.

Footnotes

(1) Trinity, a famous monastery, pilgrimage to which is reckoned a virtue. Avdyeitch calls this zemlyak-starichok, Bozhi chelovyek, God's man.—Ed.

(2) Traktir.

(3) Cabbage-soup.

(4) Gruel.

(5) House-porter.

(6) Valenki.

(7) To signify he was satisfied; a custom among the Russians.—Ed.

(8) Khozyaïn.

(9) Umnitsa aumnitsa! literally, clever one.

(10) Dvagrivennui, silver, worth sixteen cents.

(11) Diedushka.

About Author

In the 1870s Tolstoy experienced a profound moral crisis, followed by what he regarded as an equally profound spiritual awakening, as outlined in his non-fiction work A Confession (1882). His literal interpretation of the ethical teachings of Jesus, centering on the Sermon on the Mount, caused him to become a fervent Christian anarchist and pacifist. Tolstoy's ideas on nonviolent resistance, expressed in such works as The Kingdom of God Is Within You (1894), were to have a profound impact on such pivotal 20th-century figures as Mahatma Gandhi and Martin Luther King Jr. Tolstoy also became a dedicated advocate of Georgism, the economic philosophy of Henry George, which he incorporated into his writing, particularly Resurrection (1899).

Origins

The Tolstoys were a well-known family of old Russian nobility who traced their ancestry to a mythical nobleman named Indris described by Pyotr Tolstoy as arriving "from Nemec, from the lands of Caesar" to Chernigov in 1353 along with his two sons Litvinos (or Litvonis) and Zimonten (or Zigmont) and a druzhina of 3000 people. While the word "Nemec" has been long used to describe Germans only, at that time it was applied to any foreigner who didn't speak Russian (from the word nemoy meaning mute). Indris was then converted to Eastern Orthodoxy under the name of Leonty and his sons – as Konstantin and Feodor, respectively. Konstantin's grandson Andrei Kharitonovich was nicknamed Tolstiy (translated as fat) by Vasily II of Moscow after he moved from Chernigov to Moscow.

Because of the pagan names and the fact that Chernigov at the time was ruled by Demetrius I Starshy some researches concluded that they were Lithuanians who arrived from the Grand Duchy of Lithuania, then part of the State of the Teutonic Order. At the same time, no mention of Indris was ever found in the 14th – 16th-century documents, while the Chernigov Chronicles used by Pyotr Tolstoy as a reference were lost. The first documented members of the Tolstoy family also lived during the 17th century, thus Pyotr

Tolstoy himself is generally considered the founder of the noble house, being granted the title of count by Peter the Great.

Life and career

Tolstoy was born at Yasnaya Polyana, a family estate 12 kilometres (7.5 mi) southwest of Tula, Russia, and 200 kilometers (120 mi) south of Moscow. He was the fourth of five children of Count Nikolai Ilyich Tolstoy (1794–1837), a veteran of the Patriotic War of 1812, and Countess Mariya Tolstaya (née Volkonskaya; 1790–1830). After his mother died when he was two and his father when he was nine, Tolstoy and his siblings were brought up by relatives. In 1844, he began studying law and oriental languages at Kazan University, where teachers described him as "both unable and unwilling to learn." Tolstoy left the university in the middle of his studies, returned to Yasnaya Polyana and then spent much of his time in Moscow, Tula and Saint Petersburg, leading a lax and leisurely lifestyle. He began writing during this period, including his first novel Childhood, a fictitious account of his own youth, which was published in 1852. In 1851, after running up heavy gambling debts, he went with his older brother to the Caucasus and joined the army. Tolstoy served as a young artillery officer during the Crimean War and was in Sevastopol during the 11-month-long siege of Sevastopol in 1854–55, including the Battle of the Chernaya. During the war he was recognised for his bravery and courage and promoted to lieutenant. He was appalled by the number of deaths involved in warfare, and left the army after the end of the Crimean War.

His conversion from a dissolute and privileged society author to the non-violent and spiritual anarchist of his latter days was brought about by his experience in the army as well as two trips around Europe in 1857 and 1860–61. Others who followed the same path were Alexander Herzen, Mikhail Bakunin and Peter Kropotkin. During his 1857 visit, Tolstoy witnessed a public execution in Paris, a traumatic experience that would mark the rest of his life. Writing in a letter to his friend Vasily Botkin: "The truth is that the State is a conspiracy designed not only to exploit, but above all to corrupt its citizens ... Henceforth, I shall never serve any government anywhere." Tolstoy's concept of non-violence or Ahimsa was bolstered when he read a

German version of the Tirukkural. He later instilled the concept in Mahatma Gandhi through his A Letter to a Hindu when young Gandhi corresponded with him seeking his advice.

His European trip in 1860–61 shaped both his political and literary development when he met Victor Hugo, whose literary talents Tolstoy praised after reading Hugo's newly finished Les Misérables. The similar evocation of battle scenes in Hugo's novel and Tolstoy's War and Peace indicates this influence. Tolstoy's political philosophy was also influenced by a March 1861 visit to French anarchist Pierre-Joseph Proudhon, then living in exile under an assumed name in Brussels. Apart from reviewing Proudhon's forthcoming publication, La Guerre et la Paix (War and Peace in French), whose title Tolstoy would borrow for his masterpiece, the two men discussed education, as Tolstoy wrote in his educational notebooks: "If I recount this conversation with Proudhon, it is to show that, in my personal experience, he was the only man who understood the significance of education and of the printing press in our time."

Fired by enthusiasm, Tolstoy returned to Yasnaya Polyana and founded 13 schools for the children of Russia's peasants, who had just been emancipated from serfdom in 1861. Tolstoy described the school's principles in his 1862 essay "The School at Yasnaya Polyana". Tolstoy's educational experiments were short-lived, partly due to harassment by the Tsarist secret police. However, as a direct forerunner to A.S. Neill's Summerhill School, the school at Yasnaya Polyana can justifiably be claimed the first example of a coherent theory of democratic education.

Towards the end of his career, Tolstoy was selected to receive the first Nobel Prize in Literature in 1901, but turned down the honor in October of the same year, worrying that the prize money would bring unwanted complications to his life.

Personal life

The death of his brother Nikolay in 1860 had an impact on Tolstoy, and led him to a desire to marry. On 23 September 1862, Tolstoy married Sophia Andreevna Behrs, who was 16 years his junior and the daughter of a court physician. She was called Sonya, the Russian diminutive of Sofia, by her family and friends. They had 13 children, eight of whom survived childhood:

Count Sergei Lvovich Tolstoy (1863–1947), composer and ethnomusicologist

Countess Tatyana Lvovna Tolstaya (1864–1950), wife of Mikhail Sergeevich Sukhotin

Count Ilya Lvovich Tolstoy (1866–1933), writer

Count Lev Lvovich Tolstoy (1869–1945), writer and sculptor

Countess Maria Lvovna Tolstaya (1871–1906), wife of Nikolai Leonidovich Obolensky

Count Peter Lvovich Tolstoy (1872–1873), died in infancy

Count Nikolai Lvovich Tolstoy (1874–1875), died in infancy

Countess Varvara Lvovna Tolstaya (1875–1875), died in infancy

Count Andrei Lvovich Tolstoy (1877–1916), served in the Russo-Japanese War

Count Michael Lvovich Tolstoy (1879–1944)

Count Alexei Lvovich Tolstoy (1881–1886)

Countess Alexandra Lvovna Tolstaya (1884–1979)

Count Ivan Lvovich Tolstoy (1888–1895)

The marriage was marked from the outset by sexual passion and emotional insensitivity when Tolstoy, on the eve of their marriage, gave her his diaries detailing his extensive sexual past and the fact that one of the serfs on his estate had borne him a son. Even so, their early married life was happy and allowed Tolstoy much freedom and the support system to compose War and Peace and Anna Karenina with Sonya acting as his secretary, editor, and financial manager. Sonya was copying and handwriting his epic works time after time. Tolstoy would continue editing War and Peace and had to have clean final drafts to be delivered to the publisher.

However, their later life together has been described by A.N. Wilson as one of the unhappiest in literary history. Tolstoy's relationship with his wife deteriorated as his beliefs became increasingly radical. This saw him seeking to reject his inherited and earned wealth, including the renunciation of the copyrights on his earlier works.

Some of the members of the Tolstoy family left Russia in the aftermath of the 1905 Russian Revolution and the subsequent establishment of the Soviet Union, and many of Leo Tolstoy's relatives and descendants today live in Sweden, Germany, the United Kingdom, France and the United States. Among them are Swedish jazz singer Viktoria Tolstoy and the Swedish landowner Christopher Paus, whose family owns the major estate Herresta outside Stockholm.

One of his great-great-grandsons, Vladimir Tolstoy (born 1962), is a director of the Yasnaya Polyana museum since 1994 and an adviser to the President of Russia on cultural affairs since 2012. Ilya Tolstoy's great-grandson, Pyotr Tolstoy, is a well-known Russian journalist and TV presenter as well as a State Duma deputy since 2016. His cousin Fyokla Tolstaya (born Anna Tolstaya in 1971), daughter of the acclaimed Soviet Slavist Nikita Tolstoy (ru) (1923–1996), is also a Russian journalist, TV and radio host.

Novels and fictional works

Tolstoy is considered one of the giants of Russian literature; his works include the novels War and Peace and Anna Karenina and novellas such as Hadji Murad and The Death of Ivan Ilyich.

Tolstoy's earliest works, the autobiographical novels Childhood, Boyhood, and Youth (1852–1856), tell of a rich landowner's son and his slow realization of the chasm between himself and his peasants. Though he later rejected them as sentimental, a great deal of Tolstoy's own life is revealed. They retain their relevance as accounts of the universal story of growing up.

Tolstoy served as a second lieutenant in an artillery regiment during the Crimean War, recounted in his Sevastopol Sketches. His experiences in battle helped stir his subsequent pacifism and gave him material for realistic depiction of the horrors of war in his later work.

His fiction consistently attempts to convey realistically the Russian society in which he lived. The Cossacks (1863) describes the Cossack life and people through a story of a Russian aristocrat in love with a Cossack girl. Anna Karenina (1877) tells parallel stories of an adulterous woman trapped by the conventions and falsities of society and of a philosophical landowner (much like Tolstoy), who works alongside the peasants in the fields and seeks to reform their lives. Tolstoy not only drew from his own life experiences but also created characters in his own image, such as Pierre Bezukhov and Prince Andrei in War and Peace, Levin in Anna Karenina and to some extent, Prince Nekhlyudov in Resurrection.

War and Peace is generally thought to be one of the greatest novels ever written, remarkable for its dramatic breadth and unity. Its vast canvas includes 580 characters, many historical with others fictional. The story moves from family life to the headquarters of Napoleon, from the court of Alexander I of Russia to the battlefields of Austerlitz and Borodino. Tolstoy's original idea for the novel was to investigate the causes of the Decembrist revolt, to which it refers only in the last chapters, from which can be deduced that Andrei Bolkonsky's son will become one of the Decembrists. The novel explores Tolstoy's theory of history, and in particular the insignificance of individuals such as Napoleon and Alexander. Somewhat surprisingly, Tolstoy did not consider War and Peace to be a novel (nor did he consider many of the great Russian fictions written at that time to be novels). This view becomes less surprising if one considers that Tolstoy was a novelist of the realist school who considered the novel to be a framework for the examination of social and political issues in nineteenth-century life. War and Peace (which is to Tolstoy really an epic in prose) therefore did not qualify. Tolstoy thought that Anna Karenina was his first true novel.

After Anna Karenina, Tolstoy concentrated on Christian themes, and his later novels such as The Death of Ivan Ilyich (1886) and What Is to Be Done? develop a radical anarcho-pacifist Christian philosophy which led to his excommunication from the Russian Orthodox Church in 1901. For all the praise showered on Anna Karenina and War and Peace, Tolstoy rejected the two works later in his life as something not as true of reality.

In his novel Resurrection, Tolstoy attempts to expose the injustice of man-made laws and the hypocrisy of institutionalized church. Tolstoy also explores and explains the economic philosophy of Georgism, of which he had become a very strong advocate towards the end of his life.

Tolstoy also tried himself in poetry with several soldier songs written during his military service and fairy tales in verse such as Volga-bogatyr and Oaf stylized as national folk songs. They were written between 1871 and 1874 for his Russian Book for Reading, a collection of short stories in four volumes (total of 629 stories in various genres) published along with the New Azbuka textbook and addressed to schoolchildren. Nevertheless, he was skeptical about poetry as a genre. As he famously said, "Writing poetry is like ploughing and dancing at the same time". According to Valentin Bulgakov, he criticised poets, including Alexander Pushkin, for their "false" epithets used "simply to make it rhyme".

Critical appraisal by other authors

Tolstoy's contemporaries paid him lofty tributes. Fyodor Dostoyevsky, who died thirty years before Tolstoy's death, thought him the greatest of all living novelists. Gustave Flaubert, on reading a translation of War and Peace, exclaimed, "What an artist and what a psychologist!" Anton Chekhov, who often visited Tolstoy at his country estate, wrote, "When literature possesses a Tolstoy, it is easy and pleasant to be a writer; even when you know you have achieved nothing yourself and are still achieving nothing, this is not as terrible as it might otherwise be, because Tolstoy achieves for everyone. What he does serves to justify all the hopes and aspirations invested in literature." The 19th-century British poet and critic Matthew Arnold opined that "A novel by Tolstoy is not a work of art but a piece of life."

Later novelists continued to appreciate Tolstoy's art, but sometimes also expressed criticism. Arthur Conan Doyle wrote "I am attracted by his earnestness and by his power of detail, but I am repelled by his looseness of construction and by his unreasonable and impracticable mysticism." Virginia

Woolf declared him "the greatest of all novelists." James Joyce noted that "He is never dull, never stupid, never tired, never pedantic, never theatrical!" Thomas Mann wrote of Tolstoy's seemingly guileless artistry: "Seldom did art work so much like nature." Vladimir Nabokov heaped superlatives upon The Death of Ivan Ilyich and Anna Karenina; he questioned, however, the reputation of War and Peace, and sharply criticized Resurrection and The Kreutzer Sonata.

Religious and political beliefs

After reading Schopenhauer's The World as Will and Representation, Tolstoy gradually became converted to the ascetic morality upheld in that work as the proper spiritual path for the upper classes: "Do you know what this summer has meant for me? Constant raptures over Schopenhauer and a whole series of spiritual delights which I've never experienced before. ... no student has ever studied so much on his course, and learned so much, as I have this summer"

In Chapter VI of A Confession, Tolstoy quoted the final paragraph of Schopenhauer's work. It explained how the nothingness that results from complete denial of self is only a relative nothingness, and is not to be feared. The novelist was struck by the description of Christian, Buddhist, and Hindu ascetic renunciation as being the path to holiness. After reading passages such as the following, which abound in Schopenhauer's ethical chapters, the Russian nobleman chose poverty and formal denial of the will:

But this very necessity of involuntary suffering (by poor people) for eternal salvation is also expressed by that utterance of the Savior (Matthew 19:24): "It is easier for a camel to go through the eye of a needle, than for a rich man to enter into the kingdom of God." Therefore, those who were greatly in earnest about their eternal salvation, chose voluntary poverty when fate had denied this to them and they had been born in wealth. Thus Buddha Sakyamuni was born a prince, but voluntarily took to the mendicant's staff; and Francis of Assisi, the founder of the mendicant orders who, as a youngster at a ball, where the daughters of all the notabilities were sitting together, was asked: "Now Francis, will you not soon make your choice from these beauties?"

and who replied: "I have made a far more beautiful choice!" "Whom?" "La povertà (poverty)": whereupon he abandoned every thing shortly afterwards and wandered through the land as a mendicant.

In 1884, Tolstoy wrote a book called What I Believe, in which he openly confessed his Christian beliefs. He affirmed his belief in Jesus Christ's teachings and was particularly influenced by the Sermon on the Mount, and the injunction to turn the other cheek, which he understood as a "commandment of non-resistance to evil by force" and a doctrine of pacifism and nonviolence. In his work The Kingdom of God Is Within You, he explains that he considered mistaken the Church's doctrine because they had made a "perversion" of Christ's teachings. Tolstoy also received letters from American Quakers who introduced him to the non-violence writings of Quaker Christians such as George Fox, William Penn and Jonathan Dymond. Tolstoy believed being a Christian required him to be a pacifist; the consequences of being a pacifist, and the apparently inevitable waging of war by government, are the reason why he is considered a philosophical anarchist.

Later, various versions of "Tolstoy's Bible" would be published, indicating the passages Tolstoy most relied on, specifically, the reported words of Jesus himself.

Tolstoy believed that a true Christian could find lasting happiness by striving for inner self-perfection through following the Great Commandment of loving one's neighbor and God rather than looking outward to the Church or state for guidance. His belief in nonresistance when faced by conflict is another distinct attribute of his philosophy based on Christ's teachings. By directly influencing Mahatma Gandhi with this idea through his work The Kingdom of God Is Within You (full text of English translation available on Wikisource), Tolstoy's profound influence on the nonviolent resistance movement reverberates to this day. He believed that the aristocracy were a burden on the poor, and that the only solution to how we live together is through anarchism.

He also opposed private property in land ownership and the institution of marriage and valued the ideals of chastity and sexual abstinence (discussed in Father Sergius and his preface to The Kreutzer Sonata), ideals also held by the young Gandhi. Tolstoy's later work derives a passion and verve from the depth of his austere moral views. The sequence of the temptation of Sergius in Father Sergius, for example, is among his later triumphs. Gorky relates how Tolstoy once read this passage before himself and Chekhov and that Tolstoy was moved to tears by the end of the reading. Other later passages of rare power include the personal crises that were faced by the protagonists of The Death of Ivan Ilyich, and of Master and Man, where the main character in the former or the reader in the latter are made aware of the foolishness of the protagonists' lives.

Tolstoy had a profound influence on the development of Christian anarchist thought. The Tolstoyans were a small Christian anarchist group formed by Tolstoy's companion, Vladimir Chertkov (1854–1936), to spread Tolstoy's religious teachings. Philosopher Peter Kropotkin wrote of Tolstoy in the article on anarchism in the 1911 Encyclopædia Britannica:

Without naming himself an anarchist, Leo Tolstoy, like his predecessors in the popular religious movements of the 15th and 16th centuries, Chojecki, Denk and many others, took the anarchist position as regards the state and property rights, deducing his conclusions from the general spirit of the teachings of Jesus and from the necessary dictates of reason. With all the might of his talent, Tolstoy made (especially in The Kingdom of God Is Within You) a powerful criticism of the church, the state and law altogether, and especially of the present property laws. He describes the state as the domination of the wicked ones, supported by brutal force. Robbers, he says, are far less dangerous than a well-organized government. He makes a searching criticism of the prejudices which are current now concerning the benefits conferred upon men by the church, the state, and the existing distribution of property, and from the teachings of Jesus he deduces the rule of non-resistance and the absolute condemnation of all wars. His religious arguments are, however, so well combined with arguments borrowed from a dispassionate observation of the present evils, that the anarchist portions of his works appeal to the religious and the non-religious reader alike.

During the Boxer Rebellion in China, Tolstoy praised the Boxers. He was harshly critical of the atrocities committed by the Russians, Germans, Americans, Japanese, and other western troops. He accused them of engaging in slaughter when he heard about the lootings, rapes, and murders, in what he saw as Christian brutality. Tolstoy also named the two monarchs most responsible for the atrocities; Nicholas II of Russia and Wilhelm II of Germany. Tolstoy, a famous sinophile, also read the works of Chinese thinker and philosopher, Confucius. Tolstoy corresponded with the Chinese intellectual Gu Hongming and recommended that China remain an agrarian nation and warned against reform like what Japan implemented.

The Eight-Nation Alliance intervention in the Boxer Rebellion was denounced by Tolstoy as were the Philippine–American War and the Second Boer War between the British Empire and the two independent Boer republics. The words "terrible for its injustice and cruelty" were used to describe the Czarist intervention in China by Tolstoy. Confucius's works were studied by Tolstoy. The attack on China in the Boxer Rebellion was railed against by Tolstoy. The war against China was criticized by Leonid Andreev and Gorkey. To the Chinese people, an epistle, was written by Tolstoy as part of the criticism of the war by intellectuals in Russia. The activities of Russia in China by Nicholas II were described in an open letter where they were slammed and denounced by Leo Tolstoy in 1902. Tolstoy corresponded with Gu Hongming and they both opposed the Hundred Day's Reform by Kang Youwei and agreed that the reform movement was perilous. Tolstoys' ideology on non violence shaped the anarchist thought of the Society for the Study of Socialism in China. Lao Zi and Confucius's teachings were studied by Tolstoy. Chinese Wisdom was a text written by Tolstoy. The Boxer Rebellion stirred Tolstoy's interest in Chinese philosophy. The Boxer and Boxer wars were denounced by Tolstoy.

In hundreds of essays over the last 20 years of his life, Tolstoy reiterated the anarchist critique of the state and recommended books by Kropotkin and Proudhon to his readers, whilst rejecting anarchism's espousal of violent revolutionary means. In the 1900 essay, "On Anarchy", he wrote; "The Anarchists are right in everything; in the negation of the existing order, and in the assertion that, without Authority, there could not be worse violence than that of Authority under existing conditions. They are mistaken only in thinking that Anarchy can be instituted by a revolution. But it will be instituted only by there being more and more people who do not require the protection of governmental power ... There can be only one permanent revolution—a moral one: the regeneration of the inner man." Despite his misgivings about anarchist violence, Tolstoy took risks to circulate the prohibited publications of anarchist thinkers in Russia, and corrected the proofs of Kropotkin's "Words of a Rebel", illegally published in St Petersburg in 1906.

Tolstoy was enthused by the economic thinking of Henry George, incorporating it approvingly into later works such as Resurrection (1899), the book that played a major factor in his excommunication.

In 1908, Tolstoy wrote A Letter to a Hindu outlining his belief in non-violence as a means for India to gain independence from British colonial rule. In 1909, a copy of the letter was read by Gandhi, who was working as a lawyer in South Africa at the time and just becoming an activist. Tolstoy's letter was significant for Gandhi, who wrote Tolstoy seeking proof that he was the real author, leading to further correspondence between them.

Reading Tolstoy's The Kingdom of God Is Within You also convinced Gandhi to avoid violence and espouse nonviolent resistance, a debt Gandhi acknowledged in his autobiography, calling Tolstoy "the greatest apostle of non-violence that the present age has produced". The correspondence between Tolstoy and Gandhi would only last a year, from October 1909 until Tolstoy's death in November 1910, but led Gandhi to give the name Tolstoy Colony to his second ashram in South Africa. Besides nonviolent resistance, the two men shared a common belief in the merits of vegetarianism, the subject of several of Tolstoy's essays.

Tolstoy also became a major supporter of the Esperanto movement. Tolstoy was impressed by the pacifist beliefs of the Doukhobors and brought their persecution to the attention of the international community, after they burned their weapons in peaceful protest in 1895. He aided the Doukhobors in migrating to Canada. In 1904, during the Russo-Japanese War, Tolstoy condemned the war and wrote to the Japanese Buddhist priest Soyen Shaku in a failed attempt to make a joint pacifist statement.

Towards the end of his life, Tolstoy become more and more occupied with the economic theory and social philosophy of Georgism. He spoke of great admiration of Henry George, stating once that "People do not argue with the teaching of George; they simply do not know it. And it is impossible to do otherwise with his teaching, for he who becomes acquainted with it cannot but agree." He also wrote a preface to George's Social Problems. Tolstoy and George both rejected private property in land (the most important source of income of the passive Russian aristocracy that Tolstoy so heavily criticized) whilst simultaneously both rejecting a centrally planned socialist economy. Some assume that this development in Tolstoy's thinking was a move away from his anarchist views, since Georgism requires a central administration to collect land rent and spend it on infrastructure. However, anarchist versions of Georgism have also been proposed since. Tolstoy's 1899 novel Resurrection explores his thoughts on Georgism in more detail and hints that Tolstoy indeed had such a view. It suggests the possibility of small communities with some form of local governance to manage the collective land rents for common goods; whilst still heavily criticising institutions of the state such as the justice system.

Death

Tolstoy died in 1910, at the age of 82. Just prior to his death, his health had been a concern of his family, who were actively engaged in his care on a daily basis. During his last few days, he had spoken and written about dying. Renouncing his aristocratic lifestyle, he had finally gathered the nerve to separate from his wife, and left home in the middle of winter, in the dead of night. His secretive departure was an apparent attempt to escape unannounced from Sophia's jealous tirades. She was outspokenly opposed to many of his teachings, and in recent years had grown envious of the attention which it seemed to her Tolstoy lavished upon his Tolstoyan "disciples".

Tolstoy died of pneumonia at Astapovo train station, after a day's rail journey south. The station master took Tolstoy to his apartment, and his personal doctors were called to the scene. He was given injections of morphine and camphor.

The police tried to limit access to his funeral procession, but thousands of peasants lined the streets. Still, some were heard to say that, other than knowing that "some nobleman had died", they knew little else about Tolstoy.

According to some sources, Tolstoy spent the last hours of his life preaching love, nonviolence, and Georgism to his fellow passengers on the train. (Source: Wikipedia)

CPSIA information can be obtained
at www.ICGtesting.com
Printed in the USA
BVHW030546210819
556237BV00021B/65/P

9 789353 830083